Life Line

by

Rosie Rushton

Illustrated by Karen Donnelly

You do not need to read this page – just get on with the book!

MEET THE AUTHOR - ROSIE RUSHTON

What is your favourite animal?
The horse
What is your favourite boy's name?
Alexander – my grandson's name
What is your favourite girl's name?
Nicola, Sally, Caroline – the
names of my terrific daughters

What is your favourite food?
Fish with roasted vegetables
What is your favourite music?
Classical, choral, Celine Dion
What is your favourite hobby?
Reading and country walks

MEET THE ILLUSTRATOR - KAREN DONNELLY

What is your favourite animal?
Woodlice!
What is your favourite boy's name?
Laurie
What is your favourite girl's name?
Jean

What is your favourite food?
Sausages and runny eggs
What is your favourite music?
Beck
What is your favourite hobby?
Drawing and printmaking

For Anna
who knows all about angels

Contents

Chapter 1
New Beginnings

The tall guy with the spots loomed over Skid and sneered.

"Skid? Skid? What kind of a name is that?"

Skid swallowed. This happened every time he started a new school – and he did that quite often.

The teacher would pick one of the other kids to look after him.

"This is Trevor," she would say. "But everyone calls him Skid."

He had told his Dad a zillion times not to let on about his nickname, but his Dad never took any notice of him. But then again, not many people did.

The tall guy prodded him in the ribs.

"I'm Josh, short for Joshua. Makes sense, that does. But what's with the Skid bit then?" He shouted above the din in the Year Nine classroom.

Skid wondered which story would work best this time.

"It's because of how I ski," he said, examining his bitten fingernails and trying to sound cool. "You know – whoosh! swish! and skid to a halt."

"You? Ski?" Josh didn't look convinced. "You're not big enough to ski."

Skid made a desperate effort to pull back his bony shoulders in the faint hope that the odd muscle might show itself. It didn't.

"I am so," he said.

"Anyway," insisted the big guy, chewing thoughtfully on his gum, "people don't ski in Norfolk."

"I don't do it here," said Skid patiently. "I do it in Switzerland. In the Alps."

He was suddenly very grateful that last night's fish and chips had been wrapped in the travel pages of the Sunday paper. The skiing photos had been stained with fat but still looked good.

"Neat!" Josh looked impressed and his sneer turned into a faint smile. "So are you rich then?"

Skid bit his lip. Careful. This is where it could all blow up in his face.

"My Mum is," he said and felt his chest go tight and funny, just as it always did when he mentioned his mother. "She's got this huge house in the mountains – that's where I go to ski."

"Cool!" Josh breathed. "You can hang out with me if you like."

"Thanks," said Skid eagerly. He had already sussed that Mayford High was the sort of place where a good mate would come in useful. It wasn't usually this easy to get one.

"I'm mega good at sports," boasted Josh. "I bet I could ski, no problem. You could take me to Swizzieland with you next time."

"Switzerland," said Skid.

"Whatever," said Josh.

"Well," said Skid, "maybe."

This could be difficult, but then again, he wouldn't worry just yet. On past record, his Dad would have moved on yet again before winter came.

In the corridor a bell rang.

"So what's it to be?" Josh asked. "Shopping mall? Video arcade? Café?"

"Pardon?" Skid frowned and pulled a sheet of paper from his pocket. "It says here Geography, Room 8."

"I know what it says," drawled Josh. "That doesn't mean that's what we're going to do."

"But I want to! I like geography!" The words were out before Skid could stop them.

Big mistake.

Josh looked at him gobsmacked and took a step backwards.

"You like geography? What are you – weird or something?"

Skid tried a knowing smile and thought fast.

"It's the skiing," he said. "See, I have to learn all about the mountains, so that I can find my way around in the blizzards."

Neat, he told himself. Good one, Skiddo.

"You're out of luck, then," retorted Josh. "We're doing coral reefs."

"That's OK," replied Skid. "I go scuba diving in the summer."

Chapter 2
Cassie to the Rescue

Geography was cool because they had a video of the Great Barrier Reef and Skid had been able to nod a lot, and say it was just as he remembered it.

Miss Denton had been well impressed.

Drama was even better because all they had to do was pretend to be someone else. And Skid was very good at pretending.

Maths wasn't so good because numbers and Skid didn't get on well together. He just stuck up his hand and asked questions and Mr Lovell said that it was good to have someone showing an interest for once.

But lunch break was hell.

"You didn't say you were a boffin," Josh said in a sarcastic voice. He ripped the ring pull off a can of cola with his teeth. "Right little teacher's pet, aren't you?"

Skid swallowed.

"I'm not, I ..."

"Sticking up your hand all the time and going, 'Please sir, what's that, sir? Could you explain, sir?'"

Skid gulped.

"I guess that's what your name means," chipped in Lee Fuller, who had a ring through his nose and looked like a grumpy bullock. "Skid, Skid the Sucking up kid."

He roared with laughter at his own joke.

"Swotty kid, more like," added Russell.

"Stuffy kid," chanted a third.

Skid felt his face begin to burn. He tried to back off, but two of the guys dodged behind him and blocked his escape.

"Skid, Skid the Sucking up kid!" The chorus got louder.

Suddenly another voice shouted way above the rest.

"Leave him alone! At least he's got a brain, which is more than can be said for any of you lot."

Skid turned round. He was amazed. A round, freckle-faced girl with wispy, red hair and huge, green eyes, was standing, hands on hips, glaring at the gang.

"Ignore them," she said to Skid. "They're all mouth. Mrs Tucker wants you by the way. In the library."

"Where's that?" Skid was so relieved he could hardly get the words out.

"Follow me," ordered the girl and marched purposefully towards the swing doors.

Skid followed her.

"I'm Cassie," she said brightly. "Short for Cassandra. I live near you."

Skid stopped dead in his tracks and stared at her. They'd only arrived at the end of last week. They'd parked the van in this field, dead quiet it was. Dad said it would do them a treat as there were no Nosy Parkers around to ask awkward questions.

"Where do you live?" Skid was on his guard now. Dad said you couldn't be too careful when people tried to get all matey with you.

"In the windmill," she said.

"The windmill?" Skid was gobsmacked. "You live in a windmill?"

"I said so, didn't I?" Cassie snapped.

"Yes, but ..." Skid stopped. He knew full well that just because you said something, that didn't make it true. "What windmill?"

"This is the library," said Cassie, changing the subject. "And that is old Tuckbox."

She pointed to the end of the room where there was an exceptionally circular woman in an extraordinary scarlet knitted skirt. She was wobbling around dangerously at the top of some steps.

"She's the librarian, watch out for her," warned Cassie. "You don't really ski, do you?"

"No," said Skid. "I mean, yes of course ..."

"It's OK," said Cassie. "I knew anyway. I'm good like that."

Skid gulped.

"You won't ...?"

Cassie grinned.

"Tell? Course not," she said. "Got to go now – give this to Mrs Tucker for me."

She thrust a battered library book into Skid's hands. It was ancient with loose pages, and a torn cover.

"See you!"

She waved a hand and crashed out through the double doors.

As the doors banged shut, Mrs Tucker turned, wobbled on the top step and clutched the shelf for support.

"The library is closed!" she bellowed, frowning at Skid. "Can't you read?"

She pointed to a large notice in red and green felt tip.

NOTICE

THE LIBRARY WILL BE CLOSED ON
MONDAY FROM 1P.M. UNTIL 2P.M.
NO ADMITTANCE UNDER ANY
CIRCUMSTANCES

SIGNED *Jane Tucker*

(LIBRARIAN)

"Sorry," said Skid. "Only Cassie said you wanted to see me."

"See *you*?"

Mrs Tucker sounded as if seeing Skid was the last thing she would want to do.

"Yes, Miss. Cassie said."

"Cassie? Cassie who?"

Skid thought that for a librarian who was supposed to be all clued up and know a lot, Mrs Tucker was really rather thick.

"Dunno, Miss. The girl with the freckles."

"Oh, very helpful!" boomed Mrs Tucker, struggling down the steps and hitching up her drooping bra strap. "There are over eleven hundred pupils in this school, several dozen with freckles, no doubt. I can't be expected to know them all."

"But she said you sent for me," insisted Skid.

"I haven't sent for anyone. I rather think this Cassie has been playing a trick on you. Now do run along."

Skid stood his ground.

"Cassie said to give you this, Miss," he said, thrusting the book at Mrs Tucker.

"Look, I don't have time now – oh, my goodness! Oh my! Oh! Oh!"

Mrs Tucker was staring at the book, her mouth so wide open that Skid could see all the silver and gold fillings in her back teeth. It was not a pretty sight.

"I don't believe it!" Mrs Tucker slumped into the nearest chair, and held the book tight to her enormous chest. "My book! It's my book! Oh joy, oh joy!"

"I'll be going then, Miss," Skid began, heading for the door. It didn't do to be left alone in a room with a woman who had just flipped.

"No, wait!" Mrs Tucker held up a hand. "Where did you find the book?"

Skid sighed.

"I told you, Miss," he said slowly as if speaking to a rather bewildered three-year-old. "Cassie had it and told me to give it to you."

Mrs Tucker looked at him closely.

"Cassie?"

"Yes, Miss."

Here we go again, he thought.

"What class is she in?"

Skid shrugged.

"Dunno, Miss."

"Well, what year, then?"

"She didn't say."

Mrs Tucker peered over the top of her glasses.

"I see," she said, in tones that suggested she clearly did not. "Well now, that is amazing. You see, this book disappeared from my desk two weeks ago. It is very special to me and the headmaster told everyone in assembly to look out for it. So why didn't you bring it back sooner?"

Skid frowned.

"She only gave it to me five minutes ago," he said.

"Indeed? Are you quite sure?"

"Well," said Skid glancing at the clock. "It might have been six minutes."

"Don't you get insolent with me, young man!" snapped Mrs Tucker. "Are you quite sure that it wasn't you who took this book in the first place?"

"No, Miss – I mean, yes, Miss, I am sure. I only got here today. I'm new."

Mrs Tucker clamped her hands over her mouth.

"Oh. Oh well, then, I'm sorry – I didn't realise. Very well – I think you had better send this Cassie to me. I want to thank her personally."

"OK," said Skid. "I'll tell her."

"You do that," agreed Mrs Tucker, and began flicking through the book.

As she did so, something fell from the pages and fluttered to the ground.

It was a tiny, white feather.

"Well!" exclaimed Mrs Tucker, picking it up and examining it closely. "A feather!"

Very observant, thought Skid.

"Thank you, angel," she went on, raising her eyes to the ceiling and smiling in the same sort of way as Skid's Dad did after too much Best Bitter.

Skid stared at her and began backing off. This woman was seriously strange.

Mrs Tucker looked up and laughed.

"Oh, I didn't mean you – er, what's your name?"

"Skid, Miss," said Skid, moving nearer the door.

"Oh, you're Skid – we were talking about you in the staff room," she said.

She beamed at him as if being discussed by the teachers was the greatest honour on earth.

Skid said nothing. He had found it was usually better that way.

"Well, Skid," she went on, "I was just thanking my guardian angel. For finding the book." She waved the feather under his nose. "They always leave a feather behind, to show you that they are there, you see."

"Right, Miss."

Weird or what?

"We all have a guardian angel, Skid. Did you know that?"

"No, Miss. That's lovely, Miss. Got to go now, Miss."

Skid shot through the double doors and didn't stop running until he reached his classroom. Life was difficult enough without having to cope with a lunatic teacher.

He was in Mrs Hooper's history class, trying to look as though he was fascinated by the French Revolution, when three thoughts struck him, wham, bam, splat!

One – Cassie wasn't in his class, so how had she known that he had a brain and come to his rescue when Josh and the gang got all up themselves?

Maybe she was telepathic.

Not.

Two – How did she know that he pretended to be the whiz kid of the slopes?

Maybe she had very acute hearing.

Hardly.

And three – Why hadn't she wanted to hand the book back to the mad Tucker herself?

Maybe she made it a point to avoid crazy teachers. More likely.

Or perhaps she was a thief and had stolen the book. But she didn't look like the kind of person who would steal things.

Then again, he didn't look like a kid who told stories because no one wanted to listen when he told the truth.

Mum hadn't looked like someone who would just walk out one day without even kissing him goodbye – and never come back.

You couldn't rely on the way people looked. And you couldn't rely on what they told you. He knew that.

He'd tell her. Let her know that he had seen straight through her.

He'd do it the very next time he saw her.

Chapter 3
A Close Shave

He didn't see her all afternoon. She wasn't in his English set and she wasn't at Chemistry. Unfortunately, Josh and Lee were.

"Hey you!" Josh grabbed his sleeve as he set up his Bunsen burner. "Mr Lovell says you're a traveller. True or not true?"

Skid felt sick. And said nothing.

"My friend," said Lee, grabbing the other sleeve, "spoke to you."

Skid swallowed.

"Well," he said fixing a smile on his face. He tried to make all his limbs go limp like you were supposed to when you had injections. "I guess you could put it that way. I do travel a lot. Australia, America, France ..."

"Oh yeah?" Josh did not appear convinced. "So what's with you living in a caravan, then?"

Sugar. Why couldn't teachers keep their mouths shut?

"Oh that!" Skid leaned against the table and tried to look laid back. "That's on account of my Dad building the new house."

"House?" Lee frowned.

"Oh yes," said Skid, warming to his theme. "We've bought this huge field, see, and Dad's building this amazing place – five bedrooms, games room, swimming pool – the lot."

Josh chewed his lip.

Lee frowned.

"That's why we live in a caravan," he said. "Just until ..."

A loud thud interrupted him. It was the teacher thumping his fist on the desk.

"You three! Stop talking and get working! Now!"

Josh scowled.

Lee sighed.

Skid sent up a silent prayer of thanks.

Cassie wasn't in the locker room after school. She wasn't outside in the playground, but Josh and Lee were hanging around there.

"Going home then, Skid?"

Skid nodded and quickened his pace.

"We'll come with you," said Lee, matching his stride to Skid's. "Fancy a change of scene, don't we, Josh?"

"You can't!" Skid exclaimed.

"We can do anything we like," declared Josh, falling in beside him. "And right now, what we like is to come home with you."

Skid screwed up his face and willed his brain to come up with a very good idea very fast.

"Well, the thing is," he began, "my Dad will be working and he gets mega angry if he's disturbed."

"So we'll be quiet," said Lee. "Which bus?"

He paused by the row of double-deckers waiting at the school gates to ferry kids home.

Skid hesitated. He needed the number nine bus – but he didn't need Lee and Josh to come with him. They would be sure to tell everyone in the entire school that Skid Tulley lived in a clapped out old caravan in the corner of a field spattered with cow pats and rabbit holes, with no sign of a building site.

He nibbled right through his thumbnail in an attempt to think straight. Then out of the corner of his eye he saw someone wobbling along on a bicycle waving frantically at him. It was Cassie.

He raised his arm and waved back.

"That one?" said Josh.

He followed the direction of Skid's arm and headed for the first bus in the row. "Come on Lee, the number fourteen. Hurry, it's just leaving."

The two guys sprinted forward and leapt on to the bus, just as it pulled away from the parking bay. The doors closed.

Skid wasn't quite sure what had happened, but he was very thankful that it had. He waited until the bus had gone and then looked round for Cassie.

"Want a ride home?" She suddenly appeared at his left elbow, slightly out of breath and with her hair blown all over the place. "Hop on."

"Thanks."

Skid was on the bicycle before he realised what he was doing.

"Well, that got rid of them," said Cassie, pedalling away at great speed from the school. "Not that I can keep running around sorting out your messes for you."

"I beg your pardon?"

"Well," she said, swerving to avoid a pothole in the road, "I got you out of that tight corner this morning, didn't I? Got you a breathing space in the library ..."

"And talking of that," interrupted Skid, "I nearly got accused of stealing that book."

"Nearly – but not quite," said Cassie, totally unfazed.

"You took it, didn't you?" demanded Skid. "You nicked it."

"I did no such thing!" Cassie turned her head and almost collided with a lamp post. "I found it. And thought it might come in handy. Which it did."

She spun the bicycle round a corner and Skid realised that they were closer than he thought to the field where the van was parked.

"You can drop me here," he said, tapping Cassie on the shoulder.

"Why?" replied Cassie. "The van's over the bridge."

So she did know.

Sugar.

"Yes," he said airily. "In the field where our house is going to be."

"Oh, don't try that nonsense on me," said Cassie. "You're wasting your breath. It's all lies."

Skid's stomach did the sort of triple somersault that you get when you ride a roller coaster after eating candyfloss and a double chocolate chip ice cream.

"It's …"

He stopped. It was. And suddenly he knew that with Cassie there was no point pretending. She knew too much.

Well, two could play at that game.

"And you don't live in a windmill!" he shouted, jumping off the bicycle and glaring at her.

"Prove it!" she taunted and pedalled off.

"I will!" screamed Skid. "I jolly well flaming will!"

Chapter 4
Home from Home

When Skid got back to the caravan, it was empty. This did not surprise him.

At four o'clock in the afternoon his Dad might be walking round town looking for Mum, or in the bookies losing money, or sitting in the *Rat and Parrot* drinking too much because he had lost money and hadn't found Mum. Every time his father watched TV and caught a glimpse of a woman with a blue anorak and long hair, they set off again and followed the trail to look for Mum. That's why they had come to Norfolk.

On *Hi Ho! Holiday* the week before, the camera had panned past a woman clambering on to a motor boat on the Broads. His Dad had leapt out of his chair, thumped Skid on the back, cried "Found her!", and started packing up

the van. He was ready to leave Warrington and follow the trail to look for Mum. They'd been doing it for two years and they still hadn't found her.

Skid sighed and glanced round the caravan. Even if a miracle did happen would Mum want to come back to all this? The chipped table in the middle of the van was littered with dirty coffee mugs. There were plates with the grotty remains of breakfast lingering round the rims and newspapers folded to the racing pages. Dad had scribbled remarks like 'Dead cert, this one!' or '£2 each way?' all over them. Skid had tried to get him to stop gambling, but Dad just smiled and said he had to make some money so that when Mum came home he could buy her nice things. The trouble was that Dad wasn't very good at choosing the right horses and had to have a lot of beer to make him feel less guilty at wasting the money he did have.

Not that he was a layabout, not like some people said he was. He made Skid clean his teeth and wash his shirts and read books from the library. He said that if Skid worked hard and learnt a lot, he would make something of himself. Then when Skid had a wife, she wouldn't go off like Mum had done – gone off and left him holding the baby. Well, *one* of the babies anyway. Skid. Mum took the other two, Tiffany and Shannon, with her.

Skid sighed and began gathering up the dirty dishes. He knew why he got left behind when Mum went off, taking Tiffany and Shannon with her. They belonged to his Mum and her first husband.

Then his Mum married Oscar and had Skid. Skid was Oscar's kid. That's where he got his nickname from, Oscar'*s kid*. But Mum hadn't liked Dad a great deal – and she hadn't cared much for Skid either.

"Him? Oh, he's a pain, that one! Well, he would be. He's Oscar's kid."

She had said it so often that when he was little, he had thought Skid was his name, and it stuck.

Mum didn't stick though. She came and went, went and came back, until when he was eleven years and three days old, she left for good.

Of course, Skid didn't tell people that. Well, would you want people to know that your mother didn't want you? Exactly. Anyway, he thought, she was probably really sorry by now. She was probably trying ever so hard to get in touch with them. He turned on the tap and watched as a muddy trickle of water lapped its way over the plates in the sink. Only she couldn't get in touch, because they were always on the move.

That would explain it all.

As he wiped the table and dried the plates and piled the newspapers under the bench, he kept thinking about his Mum. He wished he lived in an ordinary house with a proper bedroom, instead of a creaking bunk with only a Superman curtain to separate it from the rest of the van. Skid had liked Superman when he was a kid but it was pretty naff for someone of fourteen. Everyone else he knew lived in bungalows or flats or houses with next door neighbours. They said "Hi, how are you?" every morning to fathers who had proper jobs in offices and pay packets at the end of the month. Everyone, he thought with a start, except Cassie.

He didn't have a clue about what Cassie's Dad did – but at least she lived somewhere almost as odd as he did. Or that's what she told him. Of course, she was probably lying.

Even now she was probably sitting in some tidy semi-detached house. She would be giggling to herself that she had fooled Skid. Her Mum would be cooking her a proper tea with baked beans and home-made chocolate cake.

Suddenly, tidying up the van didn't seem important any more. He grabbed his jacket from the bench where he had hurled it and shoved his arms into the sleeves. He was going to find this windmill, no matter what.

If it existed.

Which of course it didn't.

And tomorrow, he would tell Cassie that he knew she was a liar too.

Just like him.

Chapter 5
Cassie's Windmill

It wasn't until Skid had reached the bend in the lane that he realised that he did not have a clue where Cassie's windmill was supposed to be. She had pedalled off towards the crossroads, and he guessed that he might as well go in that direction as anywhere else.

He was quite sure that he wouldn't find anything which was why the signpost came as a bit of a shock.

"The Old Mill, ¼ mile", he read out loud, peering at the worn lettering on the rickety wooden post.

He broke into a run and headed off down the muddy track, past a field of cows, over a stone bridge and round a bend.

And then he stopped dead and stared.

On the other side of a five-barred gate, silhouetted against the late afternoon sky, was a windmill. He hadn't expected to find one, but looking at it, he knew that Cassie had been spinning him a story.

No one could possibly live there, not by any stretch of the imagination.

It was a burnt out, empty shell.

One of its sails was smashed and hung limply, like a broken arm. Where there had once been windows, there were gaping holes like sockets without eyes in them.

Skid climbed over the gate, and picked his way through the mud. Three steps led up to the mill door.

He pushed it open and walked in.

Chapter 6
A Sad Discovery

Now he understood.

Cassie must have been to the mill and made up a story about living here. Someone had lived there, once upon a time. The floor was littered with bits of broken china and a melted, twisted metal clock lay on the top step. There were two blackened armchairs with their stuffing spilling out. They were pushed upside down against the side wall. And leaning against the wall of the windmill was an old bicycle. Its tyres were flat and its scarlet paint was peeling and rusted.

Skid sat on the top step, wondering why he suddenly felt sad. After all, it didn't matter to him that the place was a total wreck, and he certainly couldn't care less that Cassie didn't live there. Except that she was nice, and for just a little while he had thought they might, just possibly, get to be friends.

He didn't have a lot of those. And now it seemed that Cassie had been having him on all the time. She had tricked him into believing her stories and was probably waiting right now to tease him in front of the whole class at school tomorrow.

Well, stuff her. He wouldn't let on that he'd been here, he would pretend he couldn't be bothered with her.

He stood up and brushed the dust from the old building off his jacket. As he did so, a small, fluffy, white feather drifted down and landed on his left shoe. He was about to flick it off with his finger when he remembered what that crazy Tucker woman had said. He frowned and stared at the feather and then, realising that he was being as dumb as she was, he tossed it away.

Angels indeed! It seemed like everyone in the world had started telling silly stories just the way he did.

The thought should have made him feel better.

But it didn't.

Chapter 7
Time for the Truth

The next day, Josh and Lee were waiting for him outside the classroom. They were not happy. In fact, they were really, really mad.

"You needn't think you are going to get away with it!" Josh snarled.

Skid swallowed.

"With what?" he asked.

"You know with what!" spat Lee, stepping closer to Skid and curling his lip. "Sending us off on the wrong bus."

"I didn't mean to," began Skid hastily. "I'm sorry."

"Oh, you will be," Josh assured him. "Very sorry. Unless, of course, you make it up to us."

"What do you mean?" asked Skid nervously.

"See, my friend and I got stranded in the middle of nowhere," continued Lee, poking Skid in the shoulder. "Had to walk for miles to get home, didn't we, Josh?"

"We did," nodded Josh.

"And we don't like walking, do we, Josh?"

"We don't," agreed Josh. "Which is why we want to be paid for our trouble. Five pounds should do it, I reckon."

Skid gasped.

"I haven't got five pounds," he blurted out. "Honestly, I haven't."

"Then," said Lee, as the bell rang for first period, "you had better get it, hadn't you. And quickly."

"That's right," added Josh. "And what's more, Lee and me are going to make sure you do. You can count on it."

With that, they made a rather rude sign at Skid and pushed their way into the classroom.

All through Geography, Skid tried to convince himself that they didn't mean it.

All through French, he told himself that they were just trying to scare him.

In the middle of Biology, he realised that they had succeeded.

Skid looked for Cassie at lunch time, but she was nowhere to be seen.

"Have you seen Cassie?" he asked Poppy Ingram.

Poppy's mouth dropped open.

"What do you mean?" she gasped.

"Cassie – have you seen her around?"

Poppy got up and pushed him.

"That's a horrible thing to say!" she shouted, "after everything that's happened to Cassie."

She stormed out of the room, her ponytail bouncing in indignation.

Skid sighed. It might not be such a bad thing if his Dad decided to move on yet again. Everyone in this place was stark raving mad.

Josh and Lee were waiting for him at the end of afternoon school.

"Going home, Skid?" asked Lee.

Skid nodded.

"We're coming with you," said Josh, falling in step beside him. "And this time, you're not going to play any tricks on us."

Skid's heart sank. Josh grabbed his left arm and Lee gripped his right arm.

"Just move," they said in unison.

Skid moved.

This is it, thought Skid miserably, as they turned the corner at the bottom of the lane. Ten more yards and they'll see it.

Ten more yards and I've had it.

"Wow!" Lee gasped.

"Mega!" exclaimed Josh.

Skid nearly fainted.

In the middle of the field was a half-built house. A very big half-built house. In the far corner was a huge hole, lined with blue tiles and beside it a large sign said 'Swimming Pools by Splashabout Inc'. Scattered round the field were stacks of red and cream bricks and in the far corner near the caravan stood a bright yellow JCB.

And sitting on the steps of the van, waving cheerfully, was Cassie.

"Hi!" she said. "Your Dad had to go out to the town hall – he'll be back later."

Skid opened his mouth and closed it again when no sound came out.

"What for?" asked Josh.

Skid looked at Cassie who stared straight back at him.

"Oh," he said hastily, suddenly finding his voice. "Planning permission, I guess, and all that stuff."

"The police are coming too," said Cassie conversationally. "Just to check things out."

"Police?" squeaked Josh.

"Coming here?" stuttered Lee.

"See you," mumbled Josh, grabbing Lee's arm.

The two boys legged it as fast as they could up the field, into the lane and out of sight.

Skid squatted down beside Cassie.

"You lied," he said.

"True," agreed Cassie cheerfully. "But it got rid of them, didn't it?"

"And dropped me right in it," said Skid. "I mean, all this – it's not ours. What will I say when they find out?"

Cassie shrugged.

"You should have thought of that," she replied. "I didn't invent the house, you did. I just said your Dad had gone to the town hall. Which he has. That's where the police station is. He had a bit of bother with a lady in a blue coat."

Skid closed his eyes and counted to ten.

When he opened them, Cassie had gone.

*****

The policeman was quite nice really. He explained that Dad had been a bit over enthusiastic with the beer and begun cuddling a lady in the pub and calling her My Millie Love. It had all been sorted out, the policeman said, and now all Dad needed was a bit of a snooze and a nice hot cup of tea.

When Skid took the lid off the teapot, he found three feathers lying in the bottom.

He thought he should have been surprised.

But somehow he wasn't.

And when, later that evening, he dragged his Dad to the door of the caravan to look at the building work, he was somehow not all that astonished to see that not a single trace of it remained.

Chapter 8
Guardian Angel

The next morning, Skid spotted Cassie hanging around by the school gate.

"You don't live in a windmill," he told her, without even bothering to say hello first.

"I do!" Cassie protested. "Or at least, I sort of do."

She frowned and nibbled a fingernail.

"Well, you either do or you don't," retorted Skid. "And you don't, because it's all burned down and grotty and smelly."

"Stop it!" Cassie shouted at him, her huge eyes suddenly filling with tears. "Stop it, stop it, stop it!"

Skid held up his hands.

"Sorry," he said. "But you shouldn't have lied."

Cassie raised her eyebrows.

"That's rich, coming from you," she said. "I'm going."

"Going where?"

"Just going," said Cassie.

"No, don't!" exclaimed Skid. "The house – it's gone."

Cassie sighed.

"Of course it's gone," she said. "You made it up."

"But ..." Skid stopped. He didn't really know what to say.

Cassie stared at Skid.

"The thing is, you see – I tell the truth," Cassie said, "and no one ever believes me. You tell lies and everyone believes you. I reckon you got the raw deal."

Suddenly she grinned.

"Anyway," she said, "I'll see you some time."

"When?" asked Skid.

"Whenever," she said.

And with that she turned her back on him and walked down the road away from the school.

Skid didn't say anything for three days. He didn't want to drop Cassie in it. She might be weird and crazy, but she had been nice to him. If she wanted to skive off school, that was her business.

But by Friday, he missed her. Really missed her. Perhaps she was ill. Maybe he should go and see her.

"Mr Lovell, sir," he said after a particularly boring maths lesson involving triangles. "Where does Cassie live?"

Mr Lovell looked shocked.

"Cassie?" he repeated. "Cassie?"

"Yes, sir," said Skid, wondering whether insanity was catching.

"You surely don't mean Cassandra Glosset? Ginger hair, freckles?"

Skid nodded.

"But my dear boy, she's not here any more."

Skid frowned.

"What do you mean, not here?"

Mr Lovell bit his lip.

"She died. Two years ago. Such a tragedy. Such a lovely girl. It was a fire, you know."

"Fire?" The word came out as a squeak.

"Yes," nodded Mr Lovell removing his spectacles and huffing on them. "She lived ..."

"In a windmill," said Skid quietly.

Mr Lovell looked surprised.

"So you knew her, then?" he asked. "Friends, were you?"

Skid swallowed.

"Yes," he said slowly, so as not to let the sob out. "Yes, we were friends."

He didn't go to Science. He walked across the playground, behind the mobile classrooms and sat down on the old bench by the games field. He felt light-headed and shaky and ever so slightly sick.

Cassie. Oh Cassie. Why couldn't you be real?

He didn't know how long he sat there, and when someone tapped him on the shoulder he nearly jumped out of his skin.

He wheeled round to see Miss Denton standing over him, an expression of concern on her face.

"My dear Skid!" she exclaimed. "You look as if you've seen a ghost."

"I have," said Skid, although he never meant to.

Miss Denton tutted.

"Don't be so ridiculous!" she exclaimed. "Ghosts indeed! Now get to your classroom this instant!"

She turned and stomped across the playground.

Skid sighed, stood up and stuffed his hands into his pockets.

And gasped.

Slowly he pulled his hands out.

They were full of tiny, white, fluffy feathers.

And he knew Cassie had meant it. But he also knew that the next time things got sticky, it would be Cassie he thought of first.

She would see him again. Sometime. Somewhere. When he needed her.

Who is Barrington Stoke?

Barrington Stoke was a famous and much-loved story-teller. He travelled from village to village carrying a lantern to light his way. He arrived as it grew dark and when the young boys and girls of the village saw the glow of his lantern, they hurried to the central meeting place. They were full of excitement and expectation, for his stories were always wonderful.

Then Barrington Stoke set down his lantern. In the flickering light the listeners were enthralled by his tales of adventure, horror and mystery. He knew exactly what they liked best and he loved telling a good story. And another. And then another. When the lantern burned low and dawn was nearly breaking, he slipped away. He was gone by morning, only to appear the next day in some other village to tell the next story.